Koala Bare

To Jack and Tom, and all koalas, bears and Bears, with love always – JF

For Mel, my great enabler and problem solver.
To Mark and Marty, thanks for the time – MS

Angus&Robertson
An imprint of HarperCollins*Children'sBooks*, Australia

First published in Australia in 2017
by HarperCollins*Publishers* Australia Pty Limited
ABN 36 009 913 517
harpercollins.com.au

Text copyright © Jackie French 2017
Illustrations copyright © Matt Shanks 2017

HarperCollins*Publishers*
Level 13, 201 Elizabeth Street, Sydney NSW 2000, Australia
Unit D1, 63 Apollo Drive, Rosedale, Auckland 0632, New Zealand
A 53, Sector 57, Noida, UP, India
1 London Bridge Street, London SE1 9GF, United Kingdom
2 Bloor Street East, 20th floor, Toronto, Ontario M4W 1A8, Canada
195 Broadway, New York NY 10007, USA

A Cataloguing-in-Publication record is available from the National Library of Australia

ISBN 978 1 4607 5161 9

Cover and internal design by Darren Holt, HarperCollins Design Studio
The illustrations in this book were created using watercolour and pencil
Colour separation by Splitting Image, Clayton, Victoria
Printed and bound in China by RR Donnelley on 128gsm Matt Art

5 4 3 2 1   17 18 19 20

Koala Bare

Jackie French
Illustrated by Matt Shanks

Angus&Robertson
An imprint of HarperCollins*Children'sBooks*

Get this label off my toe!
You study **bears**,
so you should know ...

I may be furry,
fat and square –
but I am definitely
not a bear!

Who wants blue or yellow fur?

Grey is the colour I prefer!

Don't like picnics,

don't drink tea!

Just want leaves from my gum tree.

Some bears wear pants,

but I am bare.

Bare koalas can't be bears!

Teddy bears may feel superior,

but not when faced with my posterior.

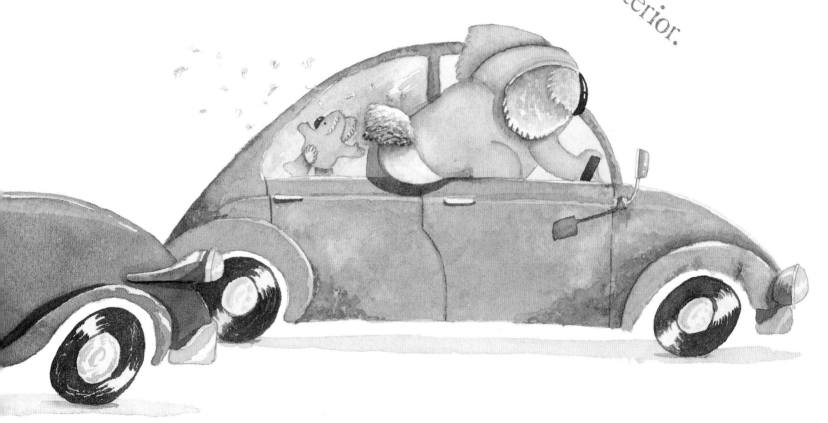

How absurd, you silly bird!

I don't need feet and giant paws

when I can climb with my sharp claws.

I just need a branch and sun.

That is

my

idea of fun.

I never,

ever

eat bamboo,

so I am not a panda, too.

Poor polar bears

must often wish

for food that doesn't **squish** like fish!

I don't need to hibernate!

Come on, now –

WAKE UP,
MATE!

Don't like porridge,

cold or hot.

Bears like honey – I do not!

Three bears living in a wood?   A cottage isn't any good!

Yes, I'm talking to you three!

Off you go,

you need a tree ...

Aren't you listening?

Don't you see?

I'm not a bear,

I'm simply ...